Saturday Night at Moody's Diner . . .
and Other Stories

Saturday Night at Moody's Diner . . .
and Other Stories

Written and Illustrated by Tim Sample

Tilbury House, Publishers

Gardiner, Maine

ISBN: 0-88448-036-4

Most of the contents of this book are derived from material originally recorded on *Downeast Standup, How To Talk Yankee,* and *Back in Spite of Popular Demand,* produced and distributed by Bert & I Records, Ipswich, Massachusetts. The author and publisher gratefully acknowledge the use of this material.

SEVENTH PRINTING
Designed on Crummett Mountain by Edith Allard

Manufactured in the United States of America

Tilbury House, Publishers
The Boston Building
132 Water Street
Gardiner, Maine 04345

Contents

I'd like to thank the following individuals who have contributed greatly to my understanding and appreciation of Maine humor: Gerald E. Lewis, Capt. Kendall Morse, Joe Perham, Alan Bemis, Rev. Robert Bryan, Steven Graham ("Unc"), Noel Stookey, and of course the late Marshall Dodge. Also a special Thank You to Robert McCloskey for advice and encouragement while I was doing the illustrations.

For my mother, Leah Sample
Who has always believed in me

About Maine Humor ...

About Maine Humor . . .

For quite a few years now, I've spent a fair amount of my spare time performin' and recordin' this "Maine Humor." I guess you'd say it comes pretty natural to me seein' as how I was born and raised here.* But lately I've noticed from the questions people ask that there seems to be some confusion as to what *exactly* this Maine Humor really is. Folks wonder, for instance, if it is humor *from* Maine, humor *about* Maine, humor *poking fun* at Maine, or maybe some combination of it all. Well, of course, I can't claim to clear up the issue entirely, but I believe I might be able to shed a little light on the subject for you.

First off, it will help if you understand a few things about Maine in general, like the fact that we've only got three categories of folks livin' here. Primarily, of course, there are Natives, that select group of individuals fortunate enough to have actually been born here in the Pine Tree State.

*All proper credentials documentin' this assertion are available from the Publisher.

The second category is made up of folks who are frequently referred to by the Natives as being From Away (Portsmouth, New Hampshire, to Antarctica and all points in between).

The third group is commonly known as Transplants, folks who originally came From Away and then decided to settle down here permanently.

You've got to understand right from the start that there's nothin' wrong with belonging to any of these categories. Where the real trouble begins is when folks that ought to be in one category, try to sneak over into another one. I'll tell you an example of what I'm talkin' about.

My next door neighbor, Wilbur Pinkham, lives in the next trailer over from mine (about four miles down the road). You can tell when you get to Wilbur's place, because it has an old Dodge 225 slant six engine block hangin' off the branch of an oak tree out front. Originally the Whipple boys had planned on doin' a valve job on that motor, but as it turned out, we had a bad spell of rain just after it was hung up, and by the time they got around to the project it was froze up solid as a log. That didn't bother Wilbur a mite. By that time he'd kind of gotten used to seein' the thing hangin' there, so he just painted it red and used it for a mailbox.

Well, at any rate, most folks hereabouts just assume that Wilbur is a Native, especially since he's ninety-seven years old and has been livin' out on this road as long as anybody can remember. But I happen to know the truth about Wilbur. He was originally born over to Keene, New Hampshire, and he was at least six months old before he ever set foot in the State of Maine.

Wilbur was over to my place for a visit a while back, and the conversation got around to the subject of his Native status.

"To be real truthful," he says, "I'm not a Native Mainer."

"I know that, Wilbur," says I.

A little bit defensive at this point, Wilbur shot back, "On the other hand, Mother and I have four grown children, all of 'em born and raised right in this town. I guess you'd have to call *them* Natives."

"Well, Wilbur," I replied, "You can call 'em anythin' you've a mind to, but I'll tell you this, if my cat was to have kittens in the oven, I wouldn't necessarily call 'em biscuits!"

Now, it would be easy to get the impression from that kind of remark that Mainers are hostile towards outsiders, but nothin' could be further from the truth. The fact is that the average Native Mainer is probably more genuinely tolerant of the diverse eccentricities of human nature then anybody on the face of the earth. What we won't stand for, however, is the attitude, either stated or implied, that being From Away somehow makes the newcomer superior to the Native. Just about anyone, from just about anywhere, can survive, even do pretty well, in Maine so long as they bear in mind that any true Native worth his salt has a finely developed natural instinct for deflating overblown egos if they should happen to stray within range.

Saturday Night at Moody's Diner . . .

Saturday Night at Moody's Diner . . .

If you plan to visit Maine in the summertime, or if you're a Native and you expect some out-of-state friends or relatives to drop by for a visit, I've got some good advice for you. The summer just won't be complete without a visit to some of our fine restaurants.

Now, as you probably know, Maine is blessed with a whole raft* of dining establishments, many of which are world-renowned for their food and atmosphere. You can enjoy spectacular sunset vistas of the rockbound shoreline while feasting on platters of lobsters, steamed clams, and fresh native corn-on-the-cob. Or perhaps you prefer a secluded mountain hideaway with that continental-type cuisine. But I can tell you right now that if you really want the ultimate dinin' experience in the Pine Tree State, you've got but one choice.

*Raft: (noun) an extremely large quantity

The place I'm referrin' to is located smack dag in the middle of Route One, gift shop capital of the universe. You pull onto Route One when you cross the Maine border in Kittery, and before you've rolled up a hundred miles you will be exposed to a greater collection of gift shops and factory outlets than most folks ever see in two lifetimes. You will find every item you ever dreamed of, and a lot of stuff you had no idea you needed until you saw it.

But we're talkin' about restaurants here, not gift shops. You keep drivin' through Wiscasset, past Damariscotta, and you'll begin to approach the town of Waldoboro. Now, Waldoboro ain't that big of a town, so you've got to keep your eyes peeled, but I'll tell you how you know you're gettin' close. When you start comin' into Waldoboro you'll find yourself headin' down this wicked* steep hill. I'm not referrin' to just a dip in the road. This hill is so steep that, dependin' on how good your brakes are, you start feelin' kind of religious about halfway down. You might even start feeling around on the dashboard for a handful of Jimmy Swaggart tapes. And what makes that hill so frightenin' in the summertime is that there is a little stream at the foot of it, and most of the time there's just enough fog comin' off that stream so you can't see the end of the hill.

Well, just trust me. If you keep on goin' you'll eventually level off and start headin' up the other side. Keep a sharp lookout and you'll see the sign just up ahead on the right, loomin' out of the fog as you approach. It's a great big orange sign with neon letters that just says MOODY'S DINER.

When you see that sign you'll know you've arrived at the finest restaurant in the State of Maine. As soon as you pull into the parkin' lot you'll feel right at home, because Moody's ain't one of them huge rambling places that you could get lost in. As a

*Wicked: (adverb) very

matter of fact, the buildin' is kind of long and narrow, just like your trailer. It even has a little wooden entryway like you have on your trailer, with a pair of them little ceramic cats grabbin' onto the outside of it like they were chasin' each other up to the roof. They've even got a couple of them exploded tires out front, just like you've got on the lawn in front of your trailer. You know the kind I mean. It's a regular tire, still mounted on the rim, but it's exploded inside out with the edges cut into jagged points, so it looks like Jughead's hat in the comics.

11

When you come in through the door at Moody's you have to take a sharp right or left turn (like I said, it's kind of long and narrow) and you set yourself down at one of them little handmade plywood booths. Them booths are built for intimate dinin'. In fact, you can't set directly across from each other or your knees are apt to bump. Once you get comfortable you'll notice that each booth has its own private little jukebox, the type where you get to hear the song that the truck driver who sat there before you wanted to hear. They've got all the classic tunes too, like *How can I miss you when you won't go away* and *How come you believed me when I told you that I loved you when you know I've been a liar all my life*. As a matter of fact, that last song is what Mother and I call Our Song.

And, of course, they have all the fine accessories you'd expect from a first-class diner, like them little plastic coffee creamers made in the shape of a cow. You know, the cow's tail is the handle, and when you lift her up by the tail, the milk spits out the cow's mouth into your coffee mug. And there's little white letters across the bottom sayin' "Ask your waitress about buyin' this." Of course, you never do. I did mention to the waitress one time, I said, "Gosh, you must sell an awful lot of these little cows." "Nope," she says, "but that fella that come through here in '63 did."

When you're settin' in the booth at Moody's, there's a narrow aisle and just across the aisle is the counter, which still has the original linoleum on it. Of course, it's worn out at regular intervals where the truckers' elbows have been settin'. The counter

ASK YOUR WAITRESS ABOUT BUYING ONE OF THESE!!

has a row of stools runnin' along it, and when you set at the booth, them stools come just about eye level to you. You'll have to remember that part, it's pertinent to the story.

Whenever Mother and I make plans to go to Moody's Diner, we always do it on a Saturday night. On Saturdays Moody's has a special which can't be beat for pure downright value anywhere in the State of Maine. It's a dinner special featuring all you can eat — homemade baked beans.

But you get a lot more for your money than just the beans. Oh, sure, they give you a good big charge* of beans to start off with, but there's also a man-sized paper cup of cole slaw made with real Miricle Whip, there's a little side plate with two of them nice big puffy homemade rolls steamin' hot right out of the microwave. And settin' alongside them rolls is one small square of what I believe to be the hardest butter on the East Coast of the United States. That butter is so hard that I'll wager you could hoist a pat of it up on the end of your knife, lean back, and drive that butter right through the roll, the plate, the table, and

13

* Charge: (noun) A large serving

everythin' else, and you wouldn't so much as put a scratch in the butter.

Then on your plate next to the beans you get two of them big bright red hot dogs. Not just pinkish lookin', you understand. I'm talkin' about the bright red kind that looks like the flares the truck drivers keep under their seats in case of emergency. Now, personally, I don't care for them hot dogs as far as eatin' em goes, but I'll always have the waitress pack 'em up for me after the meal so I can take 'em home with me. I swear there's nothin' finer than them hot dogs when you're deep trollin' for salmon. You can lace a couple of number three hooks into 'em and they'll take two or three good strikes and still hang onto the hook.

Now, Moody's is not only known for its value but its atmosphere as well. To give you some idea, I want to tell you of an incident that happened to us on this one particular Saturday night at Moody's. Mother and I had just settled in for our first round of beans when we heard a pickup truck pull in out front.

Now, you have to understand that Moody's is located just a few miles down the road from the town of Rockland, Maine, and as anyone can tell you, Rockland has been known for generations as a great fishin' village. Nowadays, of course, the fishin' ain't as great as it once was, but just the same there's still some able-bodied seamen who'll slip out for a week or two at a stretch, for a share of the catch. And whether they make much money or not, there's two things that remain constant. They tend to work up a powerful appetite, and they tend to get pretty gamey.* As a matter of fact, I've seen some of them so gamey when they walked in the door at Moody's that they set off the smoke detector.

BEEEEP, BEEEEP, BEEEEP!

*Gamey: (adjective) Foul smelling

Well, on this particular night, that pickup pulled into the parkin' lot, and we heard these three fellas get out. They stomped up the steps and opened the entryway door. There happened to be a bit of a tailwind behind 'em that evening and there was no question in anyone's mind that these boys was fishermen. And big ones too, I might add. I'd say that the smallest one of the three would dress out at close to 250 pounds. And from the way they stormed up to the counter I would say they were mighty hungry too.

As luck would have it, they decided to set on the three stools directly opposite me and Mother. And they'd barely plunked down on them stools, before they were bailin' them beans to 'em at a rate that would strain the imagination of most folks. I wasn't keepin' exact count, but I'd say they were scarfin' down three or four plateloads of them beans to our one. I've never seen the like. of it.

Now, as everyone knows, there is an inevitable physiological consequence which accompanies the consumption of a large quantity of this particular vegetable. And the effect is exacerbated when they are consumed in an enclosed environment. Not that there is anythin' wrong with it, you understand. That's just the way folks are constructed, and have been since the dawn of time, for all we know. But down through the centuries, hundreds of various techniques have been devised to deal with this potentially embarrassing problem. Now, I haven't the time or the inclination to go into all the details at this point. However, if you think about it, I believe you'll agree that virtually all of these diverse techniques for alleviatin' the excess buildup in your system would fall into one of two general categories.

Category one (generally preferred by professional people) is a technique whereby you allow this buildup to escape in such a manner that it's virtually impossible to determine that it has escaped at all. At least for a few minutes. At which point it is equally impossible to correctly affix blame.

Category Two on the other hand (generally preferred by sportsmen) is what I simply refer to as the "Let 'er Rip" approach.

Well, let me put it to you this way. There was no question in my mind that these fellas were sportsmen. The largest one of 'em, who was seated to Mother's immediate left, let go with what I would conservatively estimate to be a forty-eight-second fart that darned near blew the doors off that diner.

I'll tell you, chummy, it was pure pandemonium in that diner. There were two elderly ladies up at one end, and their teacups jumped about six inches off the table. There were a half dozen anti-nuclear types down at the other end, and they immediately leaped under the table, figurin' Wiscasset had finally blowed up. There was even a busload of school kids comin' back from an outin' at summer camp, and the bus pulled into the parkin' lot thinkin' they'd had a blowout in one of the tires. It seemed as though all creation was bustin' loose.

Of course, them boys just kept bailin' them beans to 'em just like nothin' ever happened. Everybody started lookin' up our way, Mother was gettin' kind of embarrassed at all the publicity, and frankly I felt called upon to make some sort of rebuttal. Not that I liked the idea, you understand, but Mother's honor was involved. So I stood up and tapped this fella on the shoulder. He just kept on bailin' beans. I tapped a little harder. Still no response. Finally I gathered up all my nerve and yelled at the top of my lungs, "HOW DARE YOU??!!!"

He turned around and gave me a blank stare. Seeing that I had his attention, I pressed on. "How dare you," I said, "set there on that stool and do such a thing before my wife here?" I was pointin' toward Mother as I said it. He put down his fork, turned around slowly, and looked at Mother. Then he turned back to me and said, "Gosh, if I'da knowed it was her turn, I'da let her go first."

So if you're ever steering a course for Down East Maine, and you chance to find yourself in Waldoboro on a Saturday night, you owe it to yourself to check out Moody's Diner. The food is second to none, the atmosphere is cozy, and of course the entertainment runs twenty-four hours a day.

Unc's Store . . .

My uncle runs one of them little Maine country stores up in the town of Eastport. I don't know if you've ever had the pleasure of visitin' that particular village, but if you haven't, you ought to. Believe me, it's worth the trip. A word of caution before you start out, though. If you plan to spend any amount of time in Eastport you should be sure to bring some money with you, because you ain't apt to find any growin' wild up that way.

The town of Eastport has fallen on some hard times since the big economic boom around the turn of the century. It's still one of the loveliest spots in the state, but as Unc always says, "If you could buy a Greyhound bus ticket with a food stamp, we'd all be gone outta here."

Of course, Unc has a reputation for sayin' that type of thing. It's not that he's mean or anythin'. You just get a certain viewpoint on life after runnin' one of them stores as long as he has. It's a nice little place just like a hundred others you're apt to encounter on Maine's back roads. Just a grey clapboard buildin' with a white tin sign up over the porch sayin' UNC'S STORE. There's two big windows facin' the road, and printed on each window in white plastic letters are the words ETLE TE. That's exactly what it says right on each window, ETLE TE. Now, folks come from away, and they look at that writin' and think it's pretty weird, some type of secret code or somethin'. But the locals realize that it used to say TETLEY TEA and some of them letters just peeled off over the years. That's the way it is in Down East Maine. There's an explanation for just about everythin'. The trouble is most folks don't know what it is.

Which brings me to another interestin' aspect of life in Maine. When you come up here and start askin' questions among the Natives, you're pretty apt to find that it's not so much what they say that you have to pay attention to, it's what they leave out. I remember this particular day one summer I was workin' for Unc up at the store. I believe it must have been about three o'clock in the afternoon, because we had just got done watchin' *As the World Twirled* on that little T.V. behind the counter. Not that we were all that interested in soap operas, it's just that you don't have a lot of options as to what you watch. Eastport, you see, ain't "cable ready." We only get two stations that come in any good. We get one of the Bangor stations, the one with all the old movies and the Slim Whitman record advertisements. I've always wondered how Slim Whitman sold forty million records before I'd ever heard of him. That's one of the great mysteries of life as far as I'm concerned. The only other station we get is the low-power public-access station from East Millinocket. They have a video camera mounted up in one corner of the paper mill. It's aimed down at the floor so you get to see who's workin' what shift and so forth. If you don't come from that town, it's not all that interestin'. I'll usually switch channels after three or four hours.

Well, at any rate, on this particular afternoon, I was inside restockin' the shelves while Unc set out on the porch for his after-noon nap. There's a lot of work to stockin' shelves in them little stores. You've got to have a whole variety of items designed to appeal to all types of folks. But there's one thing I can't seem to get used to. You see it in every one of them country stores. You walk in the door and glance around and it's bound to catch your eye. Generally it's on the counter next to the cash register, a jar half full of this murky lookin' water, and floatin' in that water you'll see about a half dozen pickled eggs. How anyone could eat one of them nasty things is beyond me. Whenever I see a jar of pickled eggs it brings to mind all sorts of uncomfortable questions. Who ate the last one? In what year? What did they use to fish 'em out with? Those sort of questions are hard to ignore. I told Unc once.

"Unc," I says, "I believe, if I was starvin' to death on a desert island, and I crawled up over a sand dune and seen a jar of them pickled eggs, I'd turn right around and crawl in the other direction."

"I know what you mean," says Unc. "I'd munch down a whole box of Slim Jims at one settin' fore I'd tackle even *one* of them nasty ol' pickled eggs."

Well, as I say, Unc was takin' his afternoon nap out on the porch. He was settin' in his rocker in the afternoon sun, and right next to him was this mongrel dog name of Queenie that hangs around the store lookin' for handouts in the summer. There they were, the two of 'em sleepin' like babies, when this big car pulled up out front. Biggest car I ever saw. It was half again as long as a good-sized dory, with them fake wire wheels shinin' in the sun and all. I couldn't get a look at the license plates, but it was obviously from someplace out west. Most likely Massachusetts.

When the driver rolled his window down I got a pretty good look at him. A mighty impressive fella too. Fancy jacket, silk tie, big diamond rings on every finger. At first glance I thought he

AHEM... ..ER...DOES YOUR DOG BITE?

might be an Amway salesman. Then he yells out the window at Unc. "Hey, old timer," he yells.

Unc opened one eye, and you could see even at this early stage he wasn't enjoyin' the conversation.

"Ayuh," says Unc.

"I just thought I'd check with you before I got out of the car. Can you tell me, does your dog bite?"

Unc took a long look at the fella. Then he took another long look at old Queenie sleepin' on the porch next to his rocker.

"Nope," he says, "my dog don't bite."

Encouraged by this, the gentleman opened his car door and headed for the front steps. He'd barely hit that first step when old Queenie jumped up, barkin' and growlin', and tore into the fellow with a vengeance. He high-tailed it back to his car with the dog muckled firmly onto his leg. He shook her loose and jumped inside. Then he just sat there glarin' at Unc from the driver's seat. You could tell he was quite put out. Finally he lowered the window just a crack and yelled up at Unc, "I thought you said your dog don't bite!" "Well," says Unc, "mine don't. But ol' Queenie there sure does."

As that fella drove off in a cloud of dust, I'm sure he felt as though he had been unfairly taken advantage of and maybe even singled out for abuse. But the truth is he just happened to be the latest in a long stream of passersby who had run afoul of Unc's wit. Another example happened back in the Hippy days of the sixties.

I remember it was fairly late one evenin' and this Hippy van pulled up out front. It was an awful lookin' thing, bright orange with peace signs and flowers and stuff spray-painted from one end of it to the other. Two Hippies with long hair, love beads, earrings, sandals, and so forth climbed out and came into the store. They poked around a bit and then asked Unc if he had any Grateful Dead tapes. Unc said he'd check, but the closest thing he could find was *Ernest Tubb's Greatest Hits*, which didn't seem to interest 'em too much. They poked around a few more minutes and finally the tall one says to Unc, "I don't suppose you've got any live entertainment in this town?" "Well," says Unc, "looks like we do now."

By this time you're apt to be gettin' the impression that Unc is a real hard-hearted type of individual, but nothin' could be further from the truth. As a matter of fact, he's probably one of the most generous public-spirited folks you'll ever run across. There's even been a few times when his generosity got him into trouble.

In the old days Unc took great pride in decoratin' the store for the Christmas season. He'd plan all year long how he was gonna improve his display. One August afternoon he was flippin' through a gift catalog when he stumbled upon the perfect centerpiece for the coming Christmas time. It was advertised as a "semi-life-size genuine styrofoam sculpture of Santa and his eight reindeer," complete with mountin' hardware and lightin' for a dramatic rooftop display. Well, once Unc saw that, he just had to order one for the roof of the store.

He sent right away, and even though the ad said to "allow six to eight months for delivery after your check clears," it arrived just a few weeks later. It was so impressive that Unc had all he could do to keep from puttin' it up that day (September 25th), but he decided to hold off at least until after Halloween. November

1st dawned clear and cold, and Unc was up on the roof of the store bright and early installin' his display. By about four in the afternoon it was all in place, and everyone agreed it was the fanciest thing they'd seen around here in years. When sundown came, Unc flipped on the roof-mounted floodlights and the effect was real breathtakin'. In a matter of hours folks from all over stopped out in front of the store gazin' up at that marvelous display.

In the next few days it got real chilly, and we had at least an inch or two of new snow each day. Even though Thanksgiving was still three weeks off, it seemed the whole town was gettin' into the Christmas spirit. Entire families would load into their pickups and drive down to the store at dusk. They'd just set there drinkin' Moxie and eatin' cheese nips as the snowflakes drifted down around 'em. When the sun went down, Unc would step out onto the porch, wave at the crowd, and flip the switch that lit them floodlights. The crowd would cheer and honk their horns. It was quite a spectacle.

Then one night disaster struck. It was a Friday night near closin' time, and we were inside cleanin' up when we heard a big car pull up out front. The doors opened up and several men got out. They were hollerin' an carryin' on in such a way that we just naturally assumed it was a carload of them out-of-state hunters. They drive all the way to Maine lookin' for deer, but they usually find a good deal more beer than deer.

Next thing you know they quieted right down. Then we heard some noise like they was rummagin' around in the trunk lookin' for somethin'. And then all Hell seemed to break loose. Gunshots started blasting every which way. Unc and I dove under the counter, knockin' over a whole rack of girlie air fresheners right on top of us. We lay there scared to death until the gunshots stopped, and by and by we heard that cars' engine start and the whole crew of 'em just drove off down the road. We lay there another minute or so until we were pretty sure they wouldn't be back.

Slowly we got up and went out front to see what the damage was. From the tracks in the snow you could fairly well piece together what had happened. Looked like there were about eight of them hunters in that car. Apparently when they got out and looked up, they mistook them styrofoam deer for the real thing and started blastin' away at 'em with everythin' they had. Now, as I've said before, Unc is a pretty reasonable man and truthfully it didn't bother him so much that those fellas shot up his display like that. But what really got him upset was that once they'd

blasted the deer to pieces, they proceeded to climb up on the roof, drag 'em down, strap 'em onto the fenders of their car, and head on down the road with 'em.

I tried my best to console him. "Look at it this way, Unc," I said. "Somewhere down in New Jersey there's bound to be a freezer load of styrofoam marked 'deer meat.'"

Unc just grinned, comforted by the thought that he'd still get the last laugh after all.

Our Boy Hubert . . .

Our Boy Hubert . . .

I don't know as I've ever introduced you to our boy Hubert. It's a little bit hard to really describe Hubert. For one thing, he lives in the barn out behind the trailer. He sleeps in a 1958 DeSoto that he reconverted into a bedroom. One thing I'll say for Hubert, though, is that he's real good with his hands. He's numb as a hake, but he *is* good with his hands. You heard of folks who don't know nothin'? Well, Hubert don't even suspect nothin'.

You'll always find Hubert tinkerin' around on some mysterious project or other. Like this last summer he was hard at work rebuildin' the engine of our old Dodge pickup so it would run on sawdust and hen dressin', which are real abundant natural resources out our way. It was a hot afternoon, and I was inside takin' a nap on the couch when I heard this explosion that sounded like a nuclear bomb going off out by the barn. I dashed out the door and ran around back expectin' somethin' horrible. When I got out there all there was left of that old pickup truck was the

four wheels and the bare carcass. I glanced around without seein' hide nor hair of poor Hubert. Just then I heard a rustlin' noise up above my head, and glancin' up, I saw Hubert caught about thirty feet up in the branches of the old maple tree. He was covered with soot, but he appeared to be all in one piece, and I noticed that he was still holdin' the steering wheel from the pickup. "Have a bad accident, son?" I queried. "No, thanks," he hollered back, "I just had one."

Mother and I do worry sometimes about Hubert. He's real clever with them inventions of his, but he can't seem to make any money with 'em. We figured it was just a matter of time before the right project came along, and sure enough one day it did.

Once a year Mother and I take a trip down to Portland, to do our Christmas shoppin' and just see the sights. On our last visit to the city we noticed a whole bunch of these video game parlors. It seemed as though there was one on every street corner. Out of curiosity we poked into one of 'em. It was dark as a closet shelf in there. All the games were lit up with pictures of rocket ships and dragons and Lord knows what all else. But the thing that struck me the most was the amount of cash them kids were pourin' into them machines.

After we left I couldn't help but think that somebody could make a lot of money by designin' one of them games specially for Maine kids. Instead of all these crazy space things, it could have somethin' runnin' around the screen that our local Maine kids could relate to.

It was just the project for Hubert. We explained the idea to him, and he set to workin' on it the next mornin'. For the better part of two weeks you could hear Hubert thrashin', clankin', and mutterin' to himself out there in the barn, pretty near around the clock. Finally he came in one afternoon and told us the thing was finished. We hurried right out behind him, and as soon as we stepped inside the barn I could see Hubert had done a wicked fine job on this one.

The outside of Hubert's video game wasn't all cluttered up with these weird paintings. The whole thing was just nice weathered barnboard (of course, bein' a little damp that day, it smelled a bit like hen dressin'). The screen was from an old Philco T.V., and all the buttons and stuff were right out of that '58 DeSoto. I noticed as I looked it over carefully that there were two separate slots where you could put your money in. When I asked Hubert about this, he was real proud of himself. Bein' aware of the tourist business, he had designed the game so it would take Canadian money. "Yup," says Hubert, "she'll take that Canadian money all right. She just won't give you a whole game."

37

Then the big moment came. I stood in front of the screen and dropped my quarter in the slot. The screen lit right up, and you could see a kind of maze of twisty roads with little digital spruce trees sprinkled around the edge of 'em. Next thing I know, down from the top of the screen comes this little digital pulp truck. Looked pretty realistic too. It had half the wheels off the ground on the right corners, and every now and then a digital log would drop off the back.

I was busy watchin' them pulp trucks wind down through the roads while Hubert explained the rest of the game. When you think you've got the timin' on them trucks, like how fast they're goin', which road they take, and so forth, you push one of the buttons on either side of the machine and along the bottom of the screen runs a little digital skunk. Now, the object is to hit as many of them skunks as possible with your pulp truck before the time runs out.

It was a great idea and I was some impressed with Hubert's work. I was sure we had the ticket to fame and fortune right in our own backyard, that is, until I actually hit one of them skunks with my pulp truck. I was curious that there wasn't any noise at

the point of impact. I mentioned to Hubert that part of the fun with these games is hearin' them bells go off to let you know you've scored a hit.

"I got somethin' different for that," said Hubert, just as my nostrils filled with the unmistakable odor of fresh skunk. "Ain't that somethin', Daddy," said Hubert enthusiastically. "Don't you think that's wicked realistic?"

For a minute I couldn't say anythin'. We just stood there breathin' them fumes. Finally I turned to Hubert and put my arm around his shoulder. "Son," I says, "you done real good. You're a good boy. Particularly good with your hands. You're numb as a hake, but you *are* awful good with your hands."

The Skunk in The Well . . .

The Skunk in The Well . . .

One of the finer aspects of livin' out here on a dirt road in Palmyra, Maine, is that it provides a natural backdrop for one of my favorite pastimes, which is just settin'. When you stop to think of it, you'll realize that most folks put in a lifetime of hard work, just so eventually they can afford to go somewhere and just set. Well, my philosophy has always been that a person shouldn't put off until tomorrow the things he'd rather be doing today. With this in mind, I try to spend as much of my time as possible just settin'. I've found it extremely rewarding over the years, and I recommend it highly.

Well, on this one particular evening, I was settin' in that big lounge chair of mine, thumbin' through the latest edition of the *Valley Times*, that's our local paper which is published over to Pittsfield. It's a darned good paper too. Like it says on the masthead, "Two Minutes of the Best Reading in Central Maine."

Since it was gettin' pretty late (nearly eight-thirty) I was startin' to doze off in my chair, when Mother comes paddin' into the livin' room in that new pair of pink fuzzy slippers I bought for her down to the drugstore. Well, like I say, I was sort of driftin' off when I heard this voice say, "Honey?" Now when you're just fallin' asleep and you hear a voice callin', it tends to take on an eerie quality, like one of them science fiction movies, sort of reverberatin' around inside of your head. I didn't pay much attention till I heard it again, rather urgent and high-pitched in my left ear. "Honey?" she says, "I think the water smells kinda funny."

When I heard that, I woke right up, rememberin' that Somerset County was right in the middle of one of the worst dry spells in recent memory. Ever since May the weather had turned off dry as a Baptist picnic, and folks all around were gettin' worried about their wells goin' dry.

Sensin' the implications of her statement, I replied, "Now dear, I don't smell nothin'." Of course, that's the first thing most men will try in a situation like that. I mean, most men will try to avoid the seriousness of the matter. That's actually a good deal of the difference between men and women, you know. Women tend to pick up on this type of problem as soon as it presents itself. Whereas a man will let it build up a little bit before he takes an active interest.

Well, it was clear that Mother wasn't takin' no for an answer. She came right back at me, sayin', "I surely do smell somethin' in there that smells just like a skunk." "Is that so?" I replied, "Well, perhaps I'll take a look at it in the mornin'." That's the second thing most men will try, leavin' open the possibility that perhaps they *won't* take a look at it in the mornin'.

By this time it was apparent that Mother was bound and determined to have a look into the well, and I couldn't think of any real alternatives. Now, don't get me wrong, I love my wife, but I just didn't have a real intense desire to get up out of that lounge chair at eight-thirty at night and go pokin' around out in that well. But I could see there was no way out of it, so I finally said, "Okay, we'll go out and have a little look see."

I got my coat on, and Mother fished the flashlight out of the bottom of the closet. Now, whoever designed the flashlight knew what he was doin'. It's darned close to three feet long, and every year or so they give a batch of 'em away down to the hardware store. At first it seems like a pretty good deal, till you realize that for what it costs to fill that monster up with batteries you could have bought a half dozen regular flashlights and had change left over.

By and by, we headed out the door and started around back to the well. I was in the lead, cuttin' a path through the night with that flashlight, and Mother was paddin' right behind me in her nightrobe and them big fuzzy pink slippers.

As we approached the well (which is one of the old-fashioned hand-dug variety, rock-lined, about twenty-five feet deep), I suddenly remembered that I never did get around to puttin' a proper cap on it. As a matter of fact, the only thing coverin' it up was an old piece of odd-shaped plywood I had tossed on there temporarily about four years back. This recollection, coming upon me just as we reached the well, did not sharpen my enthusiasm for the task.

As Mother and I stood on the brink of discovery, I found it hard to stave off the one naggin' question that crept into my mind. What if there *is* a skunk in the well? But there was no turnin' back. Mother reached down and flipped over that piece of rottin' plywood, and I shined that flashlight all the way down into the blackness. I looked in, and she looked in, then I heard her gasp, "Oh, my Lawd!"

Followin' that flashlight beam to the very bottom of the well, I could see what had given her the shock. There was barely six inches of standin' water down there, and on a piece of flat rock stickin' out of it there was an unmistakable furry black and white creature. Accompanying this vision was an equally unmistakable odor, waftin' up through the night air.

We had seen enough and beat a hasty retreat back inside. Once there, Mother turned to me with that look folks get, when they've just seen one of them awful gory scenes in a horror picture. You wish you'd had the good sense to close your eyes, but since you didn't you know you'll be struck with that ugly picture rattlin' around inside your head for a good long while.

"We got to do somethin' right away," she says.

"Now, darlin'," I says, "there ain't a darn thing can be done tonight. You know it as well as I do. In the mornin' I'll take care of it."

I was doin' my best to sound confident, but she wasn't buyin' a bit of it. We went off to bed. I dozed fitfully, while she stared at the ceiling, picturin' that skunk crawlin' around down inside our well, no doubt an image more vivid than any 3-D movie.

At first light she roused me with a sharp poke in the ribs and informed me that since it was mornin' we had to do somethin'. I allowed how that was true, not havin' a clue as to what it might be. Then I struck upon an idea. "I know," I says, "I'll put in a call to Mr. Gilbert, the game warden over to Hartland. They're trained in these matters, y'know. He's probably seen this type of thing a hundred times."

I can't say I was thrilled about ringin' up the warden at five-thirty in the mornin', but one look at Mother made it clear she'd done all the waitin' she was gonna do. I dialed the number and after several rings, he came on the line, soundin' like he had eight better things to do. I apologized for the wake-up call and explained the situation as brief as I could.

"You tellin' me you got a live skunk down yer well?" says he.

"That's right," I says. "Mother and I seen him out there about eight-thirty last night."

"Did you check this mornin'?"

To tell you the truth, it had never crossed my mind to do such a thing, but seein' as how he was a professional game warden and all, I put the phone down, threw on my boots and overcoat, grabbed the flashlight, and headed out for a look. I came back about three minutes later with a report.

"Yes, sir," I says, "he's still crawlin' around down there all right. He ain't gone nowhere, and it don't look to me like he's plannin' on goin' nowhere. To tell you the truth, Mother and I are very anxious to determine the proper method of removing this type of animal from our well."

There was a long pause on the other end of the line, then finally I heard the warden's voice again.

"I'll tell you what," he says, "if you do figure that one out, you be sure and let me know."

The Tale of The Kennebeck Mariner

Holman Day was a native Maine writer, poet, and humorist whose work was published in New England around the turn of the last century. This poem, "The Tale of the Kennebec Mariner," was first published in 1900 in a collection of Holman Day poetry entitled *UP IN MAINE.* In the early part of the twentieth century Holman Day poetry was frequently memorized and recited at Grange meetings and prize speaking contests throughout New England. "The Tale of the Kennebec Mariner" is among the best known of all Holman Day pieces.

The Tale of the Kennebec Mariner

by Holman Day (from the book *UP IN MAINE*)

Guess I've never told you, sonny, of the strandin'
    and the wreck
Of the steamboat *Ezry Johnson* that run up
    the Kennebec
That was 'fore the days of steam-cars, and the
    "Johnson" filled the bill
On the route between Augusty and the town of
    Waterville

She was built old-fashioned model, with a
    bottom flat's your palm
With a paddle wheel behind her, druv' by one
    great churnin' arm.
Couldn't say that she was speedy — sploshed
    along and made a touse,
But she couldn't go much faster than a man
    could tow a house.
Still she skipped and skived tremendous, dodged
    the rocks and skun the shoals
In a way the boats of these days couldn't do to
    save their souls.
Didn't draw no 'mount of water, went on top
    instead of through.
This is how there come to happen what I'm going
    to tell to you.
Hain't no need to keep you guessin', for I
    know you won't suspect
How that thunderin' old "Ez Johnson" ever
    happened to get wrecked.

She was overdue one evenin', fog come down
      most awful thick;
'Twas about like navigating round inside a
      feather tick.
Proper caper was to anchor, but she seemed to
      run all right,
And we humped — though 'twas risky —
      kept her sloshin' through the night.

Things went on all right till morning, but along
      'bout half past three
Ship went dizzy, blind, and crazy — waves
      seemed wust I ever see.
Up she went and down she scuttered; sometimes
      seemed to stand on end,
Then she'd wallopse, sideways, crossways, in a
      way, by gosh, to send
Shivers down your spine. She'd teeter, fetch
      a spring, and take a bounce,
Then squat down, sire, on her haunches with a
      most je-roosely jounce
Folks got up and run a-screaming, forced the
      wheelhouse, grabbed at me,

Thought we'd missed Augusty landin' and
      had gone plumb out to sea.
Fairly shot me full of questions, but I said
      'twas just a blow;
Still that didn't seem to soothe 'em, for there
      warn't no wind, you know!
Yas, sir, spite of all that churnin' warn't a whisper
      of a breeze

No excuse for all that upset and those strange
        and dretful seas.
Couldn't spy a thing around us — every way
        'twas pitchy black,
And I couldn't seem to comfort them poor critters
        on my back.
Couldn't give 'em information, for 'twas dark's
        a cellar shelf;
Couldn't tell 'em nothin' 'bout it — for I
        didn't know myself.

So I gripped the "Johnson's" tiller, kept the
        rudder riggin' taut,
Kept a-praying, chawed tobacker, give her steam,
        and let her swat.
Now, my friend, jest listen steady; when the sun
        come out at four,
We warn't tossin' in the breakers off no stern
        and rock-bound shore;

But I'd missed the gol-darned river, and I swore
        this 'ere is true
I had sailed eight miles cross-country in a heavy
        autumn dew
There I was clear up in Sidney, and the tossings
        and the rolls
Simply happened 'cause we tackled several miles
        cradle knolls.
Sun come out and dried the dew up; there she
        was a stranded wreck,
And they soaked me eighteen dollars cartage to
        the Kennebec.

Trailer Life . . .

Trailer Life . . .

Everybody has their own ideas about where they'd like to live. Some like a big old farmhouse, or a little cottage by the sea, or even one of them geodesic domes. But I maintain that you've never really experienced life until you've lived in a trailer.

Now, I wouldn't have said that a few years back, but Mother's been hooked on 'em for years and she finally dragged me down to the Open House they had at St. Albans Mobile Homes over to Newport. I went mostly for the free coffee and doughnuts, but once I was there I began to get the fever.

They were havin' a special sale that week on "demos." (A demo is just like a regular trailer, except the salesman lives in it.) We took the tour, and he explained how everythin' in the trailer is coordinated right from the factory. In other words, your rugs and furniture and lamps and so forth all match up with each other, and that's important. If you stop and think about your own house or your best friends' house, you most likely realize that it's chock full of the most awful assortment of mismatched odds and ends you ever saw. Most of the furnishings in our place looked like they didn't belong in the same county with the other stuff, much less in the same room.

Well, when you buy a trailer, all that aggravation has been taken care of for you. Everything matches everything else, and it's top quality merchandise too. Even the artwork on the walls is all coordinated at the factory. And it ain't the cheap type of stuff you probably got hangin' on your walls, the type that's done on paper or canvas or somethin'. Nope, only the best in these trailers . . . genuine velvet! With your choice of all the classic themes, like Kenny Rogers sweatin', or Conquistedores, or the one that Mother really loves — a matched set of them poor little kids, with eyes about the size of large dinner plates, standin' in an alleyway holdin' a little puppy or kitty. Real art!

Well, Mother and I purchased our trailer, and we were lucky enough to get us a little piece of land where we could make sure that the slab was built real close to the road. Personally I can't see the point of havin' your trailer set way back six or eight feet from the pavement. I'd say it ain't more than three feet from my front door to the shoulder of Route Two, and the convenience is amazin'. For one thing, I hardly lifted a snow shovel last winter. Them big semis and log trucks come barrelin' by, and the wind from their passin' just blows the snow clean off the whole front lawn. And in the summertime, if I leave the windows open, them big rigs stir up such a breeze it's just like free air conditionin'.

But the real joy of trailer livin' don't come from the coordinated interior or even a prime location like we've got. The one thing that makes a man's trailer his castle is lawn ornaments.

Now, when we signed the papers on our place, we were fortunate enough to receive a year's free subscription to *Trailer Life* magazine, and the very first copy that arrived was the big annual summer lawn ornament edition.

We read that from cover to cover and learned that there's a real art to settin' up your lawn ornaments so's to get the maximum effect and enjoyment out of 'em. For one thing, you don't just go out and buy a raft of stuff and strew it around the lawn. First you have to pick a theme for your display. After thinkin' about it we decided we were gonna try "wildlife."

Our first purchase was a plastic duck and a set of little ducklings, which we positioned way down to the north end of the lawn headin' in a southerly direction. Then on the south end headed north we've got a grey styrofoam goose and these little goosies sort of aimed on a collision course with them ducks, but of course they ain't movin'. Just about dead center in between 'em we got one of them nice little cupolas. That's a rig that looks like a well house, only there's no water under it. It's made of cedar shakes, and it makes a dandy place for a half dozen of them styrofoam grey squirrels to perch.

Sprinkled around between the ducks and the geese we've got
a bunch of other little creatures, like two cement donkeys with
geraniums sproutin' out of their backs and a little ceramic frog on
a lily pad holdin' a sign that says "Welcome to our Pad." And
we've got quite a handful of them wooden willygig type
ornaments that move when the wind blows. There's four mallard
ducks with wings that rotate in the breeze, six pinwheel daisies,
and a wooden hound dog that acts like he's chasin' a rabbit every
time one of them semis drives by.

Mother had to go over to New Hampshire recently for a big
Mary Kay convention, and on the way home she stopped and
picked up some of these birds they got over there. They're a
largish sort of bird, with pink color to 'em. They've got a long
droopy neck and two real skinny legs made out of wire. I believe
the proper name for 'em is a flamenco. Well, anyhow, she picked
up about two dozen of them birds, and we've got 'em arranged in
a row runnin' pretty near the length of the trailer. Looks real sharp.

Of course about every four feet or so down the length of the
lawn we've got one of them exploded tires. Have you seen 'em?
It's a marvelous use of technology. I don't know quite how they
do it, but somehow they take a regular tire like you've got on

your car and they explode it inside out so it looks kind of like a baked potato. The edges are sawed off into a jagged pattern like Jughead's hat in the comics. The deluxe model has the tips of them jagged edges painted in opposite colors. One will be dayglow orange and so forth right clear around the tire. That might not sound too complicated or artistic, but just try it yourself sometime. I'll guarantee you'll end up with two of the same color at the end.

Of course, we had to leave room somewhere to put our lawn chairs. We've got a matched set from the K-Mart, the kind you can stretch out and take a nap in, but the lawn bein' so narrow and all we had to set 'em up facin' each other end to end. Otherwise your feet would be stickin' halfways out into the roadway. We noticed that settin' in that position it was a little difficult to see the whole lawn, so we got one of them chrome balls that reflects a panoramic view of the whole spread. There's few experiences to match settin' in them chairs just gazin' at the reflection of them magnificent ornaments in that blue ball.

Now, there's one area that sometimes get overlooked when folks are decoratin' the outside of a trailer. That's the space right around the front door. Of course, we've got a few of them round

THE HENDERSENS

cement patio blocks runnin' from the steps to the road, and right
at the end there's a mailbox shaped like Uncle Sam with his hand
stuck out. But the space I'm referrin' to is on the side of the trailer
just to the right of the front door. We've got three of them little
ceramic kittens crawlin' up the side of the trailer, and just to the
right of 'em there's a nameplate that Mother ordered from one of
them skinny little gift catalogs that comes in the mail around

Christmas time. You know the kind I mean. They specialize in items that you've never heard of before, but once you see 'em you've just got to buy one. Like them little plungers that's designed to remove your blackheads? Now, you never thought of that, but seein' it in the catalog you won't rest till you've tried one out.

Well, she ordered this nameplate from the same catalog. It's made out of "wrought plastic" (just like wrought iron, only more durable), and it has an old-fashioned carriage dragged along by a team of horses. In white letters underneath the horses it just says "The Hendersens." That ain't our name. It was a "demo" model, and I can tell you there's times when that nameplate comes in mighty handy.

For instance, let's say you're settin' inside on a quiet Saturday afternoon havin' a few beers and watchin' big-time wrestlin' on T.V. All of a sudden you hear the doorbell ring. Since you ain't expectin' anybody, you get a little put out by it. Slowly you get yourself up out of that lounge chair and open the door only to find a couple of Moonies or somebody else you don't know or care to. Well, the first thing they're apt to ask (havin' read that nameplate) is, "Is Mr. or Mrs. Hendersen at home today?" In which case you can simply say "no," shut the door, and go back to what you were doin'.

Say whatever you want. Live wherever you've a mind to. But as for Mother and I, for pure comfort, convenience, and graceful livin', we'll take our trailer any day of the week.

The Black Fly Festival...

One reason Maine is such a popular spot for folks to visit in the summertime is the wonderful variety of fairs and festivals goin' on. I've been to a lot of 'em myself. I try to make it up to Eastport every year for the vacant building festival. And of course, Mother and I wouldn't miss the Wiscasset worm days. But for pure local Maine fun and good times you've got to head up to Rangeley in the spring, for the annual Black Fly Festival.

Rangeley is one of the prettiest towns in the state, and lots of folks go up in the winter for the skiin' at Saddleback Mountain. Matter of fact, years back I used to play music in the lounges up there, always hopin' I'd get hooked up with the ski crowd. You know the ski crowd? Them young good-lookin' folks from away, that drives Porsches and got money?

To tell you the truth, I never did really hook up with the ski crowd, but I ran head on into the skidder crowd, and that's a whole different crew altogether. And the skidder crowd is the one

71

you're likely to see at the Black Fly Festival. It runs for a whole weekend with all types of events and contests, but everyone agrees that the highlight of all the activities happens on Saturday night at seven-thirty right in the center of town at the I.G.A. parkin' lot. The annual Miss Black Fly competition.

Don't get me wrong now, this Miss Black Fly competition ain't just another beauty contest. (As a matter of fact, beauty don't hardly even enter into it.) These girls are all from the skidder crowd, and they're all good strong hefty Maine girls. Last year's winner probably weighed in at about 235 pounds, and for the talent part of the competition she carved a life-size statue of Michael Jackson out of pulp wood with her chainsaw. They made a video tape of her doin' it. Only took her about an hour and it looked just like him.

In order to get a good position to see the show, Mother and I arrived down at the parkin' lot about six-thirty, and even then you could just feel the excitement. Crowds of people from all over the place was swarmin' in. Not to mention the Black Flies. The stage was a flatbed truck hung with buntin'. They had originally planned to buy a set of them big spotlights like you see at one of them gala Hollywood movie premieres. As I say, they wanted to get 'em, but I guess the town budget wouldn't stretch that far. But they did pretty good just the same. They parked the two police cruisers facing the stage and then backed 'em up so their hind wheels were down over the curb. Then the Girl Scout troop colored each headlight a different color with magic markers. When the deputies flipped them high beams on, the effect was real professional lookin'.

When seven-thirty rolled around, the three finalists walked onstage in their swimsuits and the crowd was cheerin' like mad. The M.C. announced through a bullhorn that this was serious business. Just like the Olympics, he said. The contestants had been instructed that they couldn't use any chemicals. No Off, or Ben's 100, or old-time woodsmen's fly dope. Then he stood back and the girls posed in their swimsuits. You could hear a pin drop as the whole crowd watched. Them black flies started swarmin' somethin' fierce. Finally the girl on the left broke down and swatted one of the critters and was automatically eliminated, leavin' only two standin'. Them two battled it out for the better part of three minutes until the one on the right finally gave out and started swattin' them little demons left and right. The crowd let out a cheer as the M.C. placed the Miss Black Fly crown atop the winner, knowin' that she had passed a test of stamina, endurance, and character that few people could ever match.

The Wig . . .

The Wig . . .

Old Elva Tuttle lives up on the ridge in the farmhouse his family built over a century ago. He's always been a good neighbor, but ever since his wife passed on a few years back, he's had a tendency to keep to himself a good deal. They were real close, them two, married the better part of seventy years, and he took her passin' kind of hard.

I remember the day she died. I was down to Berry's Pharmacy in Pittsfield, havin' a cup of coffee and catchin' up on the local gossip. There were two elderly ladies settin' on the stools alongside of me, and one of 'em turns to the other and says, "Did you hear that Maybelle Tuttle passed away last evenin'?" "No," says the other one, "and furthermore I don't care a thing if she did."

Well, that struck me as kinda hard-hearted, so I perked up a bit and began to listen close.

"You can't mean that!" says the first lady.

"I most certainly can," the other lady replied. "I never cared for Maybelle, and I don't care what anybody thinks of it."

"Well, at least" says the first one, "I expect you'll pay her the courtesy of attendin' the funeral."

"I will not!" came the reply. "If she ain't comin' to mine, I'm darn sure not goin' to hers."

You know, some folks are just like that, but even so I felt bad for old Elva. I knew he missed her somethin' fierce and he was just pinin' away for her month after month. So I took it upon myself to stop by once or twice a week and try to cheer him up.

One afternoon we were sippin' hard cider on his front porch and I suggested that he might try goin' out on a Saturday night to one of them dances they hold down to the Grange Hall in Palmyra village.

"You know, Elva," I ventured, "there's a number of very attractive widow ladies that goes to them shindigs. If you was to go a few times you might even meet somebody you'd like to settle down with."

I could tell right off that Elva was cool to the notion of going out socializin'. But I must say I couldn't really understand exactly why. Well, we kept talkin' as the sun went down, and several glasses of cider later I had my answer.

Once he got loosened up a bit, Elva admitted that he was a little self-conscious about his looks. He said that as he got on in years (he was eighty-seven at the time) he'd begun to notice that his hair was thinnin' out at a pretty alarmin' rate. He had his mind made up that even as lonely as he was, he couldn't take the embarrassment of askin' a lady to dance, with his old bald head hangin' out as it was. After hearin' the nature of his complaint, I knew I had a remedy.

I excused myself and went back to the trailer. I got hold of last week's copy of the *Grit* newspaper, where I remembered I'd seen this certain advertisement. I leafed through it, and sure enough there it was, a great big ad on the next to last page.

The ad was for a modern acrylic wig, one size fits all, made out of durable, weatherproof, fade resistant, acrylic fiber. It was guaranteed in writin' to make any man look twenty years younger, which would give Elva the youthful charm of a sixty-seven-year-old. Not only that, but it came complete with a tube of this new formula adhesive designed to give the wearer hours of security even in the most inclement weather. To prove this last point, they had an actual unretouched photo of a satsified customer, hangin' about six feet off the ground, suspended by a backhoe hooked onto the wig. I must admit it was pretty impressive.

I sent in the twenty bucks and had 'em deliver the goods to Elva in a plain brown wrapper so as not to arouse suspicions down to the Post Office. It came a few weeks later and I could tell I'd done the right thing when I saw Elva the followin' Saturday mornin' at the hardware store. He had that wig on, and he was grinnin' like a dog eatin' bumblebees.

About six-thirty that evenin' Mother and I were settin' out on the front porch when she says, "I guess Elva's goin' to dance down to the Grange Hall tonight." I cocked my ear in the direction of Elva's place. "Ayuh," I says, "sounds that way to me."

That part about the listenin' probably needs a bit of explainin' for folks who ain't familiar with Elva's social habits. First of all, when he goes out for the evenin' Elva always takes his horse and buggy. He claims it gets him where he wants to go and, besides, hay is a good deal cheaper than gasoline. And for an important occasion, he always douses himself quite liberally with that Four Roses toilet water. Now, I don't know what the ladies think of that stuff, but I can tell you for a fact that the deer flies are crazy over it. They swarm so thick around him that you can hear this low hummin' noise comin' from up the road even before Elva makes the crest of the hill.

By and by he pulled up out front of our place lookin' as dapper as I've ever seen him. He had on his best Sunday-go-to-meetin' suit with a fancy broad-brimmed straw hat, and you could see that wig pokin' out from under the edges of the hat. He was some old proud of that wig.

We chatted for a few minutes, and then he said he had to get goin' or he'd be late for his date. Before he left, though, I made him promise to stop by in the mornin' and let us know how the evenin' went. Off he trotted like a school kid goin' to his first social.

Next mornin' about nine o'clock Elva stopped by. I've never seen him look so downtrodden before or since. "Well," says I, "how'd everythin' go last evenin'?"

BZZZZZZZZZ
BZZZZZZZZZ
BZZZZZZZZZ

"Probably one of the worst nights I ever seen," he replied mournfully. "Oh, it started off all right. After I come by your place I headed out towards Route Two. Once I got onto the paved part and got up a little speed, I lost most of the deer flies. But when I got to the crest of the hill up there by the Palmyra Consolidated School, I slacked off the reins so's to enjoy the view. Y'know, it's a nice sight out across them cow meadows just as the sun is settin' on the hills. Well, anyways, I was sorta admirin' the view when a gust of wind come up real strong off Sebasticook Stream on my left-hand side. Next thing I knew that wind had caught the brim of my straw hat and lifted it clean off my head.

"I guess I ain't allowed enough time for the glue to set up on that new wig, 'cause when the hat blew off, it snagged onto that wig and flung it halfway out into the meadow. Now, luckily I was wearin' my trifocal glasses, but even so I have to admit they ain't got a settin' for searchin' through a cow pasture at sundown, but there was nothin' else to do but try and fetch that wig back, so I climbed down off the wagon and commenced to searchin' where I thought it might have landed. It wasn't such a pleasant pastime as I'd been lookin' forward to. But it could have been worse, I guess. After about thirty minutes of searchin' I finally found that wig, although I'll admit I tried on several before I got the right one."

The Junk of Marshall Dodge

Marshall Dodge has for many years been acknowledged as one of America's premier native humorists. As a student at Yale University in the 1950s, Marshall and fellow Yale student Robert Bryan teamed up to produce a record album entitled *Bert and I and Other Stories from Down East*. In addition to being a bestseller, this record has stood the test of time to become the benchmark of Maine dialectal humor.

In the years following the release of the first *Bert and I* record, Marshall continued to collect and record the native humor of New England.

I met Marshall Dodge in the mid 1970s, and in 1980 we began performing together in the improvisational comedy team of Sample and Dodge. During the time we spent working together, I came to know Marshall as an inveterate collector of American folk humor. His apartment on Clifford Street in Portland, Maine, was constantly cluttered with a huge collection of antique books, records, and vaudeville posters covering virtually every aspect of our native humor.

A particularly engaging aspect of Marshall's personality was his penchant for distributing these items to whomever he thought could make the best use of them.

While in the process of working on our first comedy album, I received word that Marshall had been killed in a tragic hit-and-run automobile accident while vacationing in Hawaii. In the weeks that followed I decided to try to communicate my feelings about Marshall and his contribution to the tradition of Maine humor. I eventually came up with the following poem written in the style of one of Marshall's favorite poets, turn-of-the-century Maine humorist Holman Day.

The Junk of Marshall Dodge

I'd like to take your treasures,
And your trinkets, and your junk,
And load 'em on a boxcar in nineteen steamer trunks,
And get some played-out Engineer with steam still in his veins
From a life of haulin' folks and freight
From Boston up to Maine.

And I'd stoke him with the vision
And I'd enlist him in my scheme to run that train around the
    world
Distributin' a dream.
And should he chance to ask me who might want this old hodge
    podge,
I'd say, "This ain't just any junk, my friend,
It's the junk of Marshall Dodge."

With every detail overlooked, and only grace to guide us,
We'd steam across the continent with Marshall's junk beside us.
We'd run that train to every little town along the track
And stop and draw a crowd with whistles, bells, and union jacks.

And as they started gatherin',
Men, kids, and ladies large
I'd shout into my megaphone,
Step up folks, there's no charge.
Feel free to touch the merchandise, it's more than rummage off
    some barge.
This ain't just any junk, my friends, it's the junk of Marshall
    Dodge."

With the help of my assistants
(Just recruited from the crowd)
I'd push a button on the floor
And bring the music up real loud.
Bolts would snap and locks would slide. Them trunks would
    open wide.
And men would peer, and ladies crane, to see what lay inside.

"Don't just stand there, folks," I'd tell 'em,
"Help yerself, this stuff is free!
With one small stipulation, now listen carefully.
You're free to take whatever strikes your fancy from this heap,
But only if you understand, it isn't yours to keep.

"It's only yours to spread around
and share with friend (and foe).
Now, if you can keep that promise,
Take somethin' before you go,
Like a book to send a relative
Who's homely as a stump,
Or a bicycle that's built for two
To help you o'er the humps.

"Or a tape machine to capture tales
Yer Uncle Jasper tells,
Or a boat that's called *The Bluebird Two*
To skim across the swells,
Or an anecdote to crack a smile
Across the sourest face,
Or a pin to prick the pompous
And put 'em in their place.

"It's all there for the takin', folks.
Pick well or not at all,
For there's many hamlets yet to hit while circlin' this ball.
And lots of folks along the way
In cities small and large,
Who just like you will gawk and peek
and smile
When we tell 'em (There's no charge!)
'Cause this ain't just any junk, we're handing out,
It's the junk of Marshall Dodge."